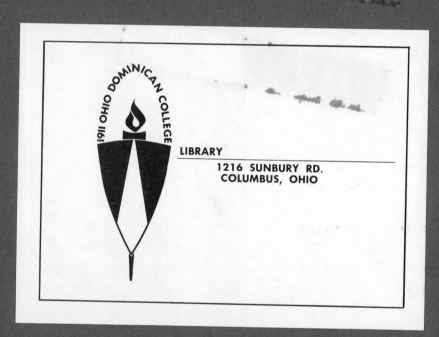

To Nancy Day, who showed me the way
—S. M.

To my father, who took us on many picnics in his yellow hatchback
—H. N.

This is the way
a baby rides.

opossums

Bump-ity bump. Don't let go!

This is the way a baby runs.

chipmunks

Quick-ity quick. High and low.

This is the way
a baby hides.

deer

Hush-ity hush. Can you see?

This is the way a baby jumps.

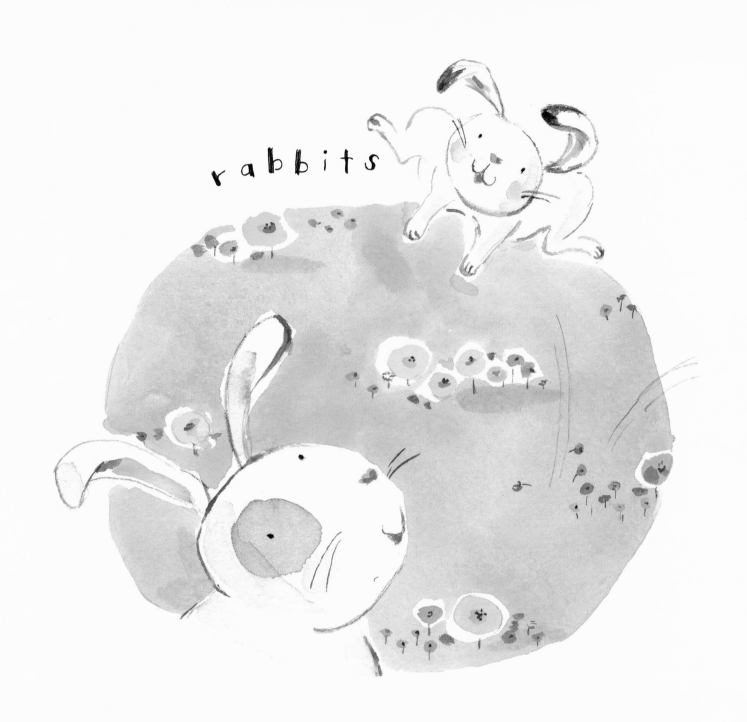

rabbits

Leap-ity leap. Look at me!

This is the way a baby cries.

birds

WAA! WAA! WAA! WAA!

Where's my lunch?

This is the way
a baby eats.

squirrels

Yumm-ity yummm. Munch and crunch.

This is the way a baby flies.

birds

Whoosh-ity whoosh. Up so high.

This is the way a baby swims.

otters

Splash-ity splash. Rub him dry.

This is the way a baby plays.

foxes

Bounce-ity bounce. Tumble, tug.

ducks

This is the way a baby sleeps.

SnoozZze-ity snoozZze. Warm and snug.

This is the way
a baby wakes.

opossums

Stretch-ity stretch. Head to toe.

This is the way a baby rides.

Bump-ity bump. Time to go.